Bo and the Christmas Bandit

Bo and the Christmas Bandit

Lynn Sheffield Simmons

ILLUSTRATED BY
ALISON DAVIS LYNE

PELICAN PUBLISHING COMPANY
GRETNA 2009

*The word "Pelican" and the depiction of a pelican
are trademarks of Pelican Publishing Company, Inc.,
and are registered in the U.S. Patent and Trademark Office.*

ISBN: 9781589807235

Printed in the United States of America
Published by Pelican Publishing Company, Inc.
1000 Burmaster Street, Gretna, Louisiana 70053

Contents

Bo and the Christmas Bandit

CHAPTER 1

The Strawberry Patch

The pleasing aroma of freshly brewed coffee combined with apple-cinnamon potpourri drifted through the store as Mrs. Barnett took her position behind the cash register. She was waiting for her first customer to enter the Strawberry Patch. The tall, middle-aged woman had arrived early to make sure everything was ready before opening the doors to the public. It was her first day on duty, and Mrs. Barnett was very excited about managing the gourmet coffee and gift shop. She and Bo, the famous black Labrador retriever known for helping police solve mysterious burglaries with his crime-sniffing nose, were in the central Texas historic town of Salado. They were visiting their friends, Ruby and Mike Cameron. During Mrs. Barnett's visit, the Camerons, who owned the Strawberry Patch, were called out of town unexpectedly. As they prepared to leave, Mrs. Barnett agreed to house-sit, and when the Camerons ran out of options in finding someone to run the store, they turned to her.

"I am sorry to ask this of you at Christmastime," Ruby had said, "but since you are so familiar with our store, and as a former teacher you have supervised any number of classrooms, will you manage the Strawberry Patch?"

Before Mrs. Barnett could reply, Ruby went on to say, "The store is well stocked with plenty of coffee and items to sell. Our employees' assignment sheets, along with their times to work, are posted for the week. I know the hours will be long this weekend. You will need to open the store at 10 a.m. and close at 9 p.m., but it is such an exciting time. Our annual Salado Christmas Stroll is well attended and has visitors coming from everywhere, even from out of state."

"Oh, my," murmured Mrs. Barnett, overwhelmed by Ruby's request. "I have attended the Stroll a number of times and have friends who come every year, but . . . I have Bo with me."

"He will be all right in our fenced yard. The weather is nice, and even at this time of the year it's not very cold."

"But you don't know Bo . . . you have flowers and shrubs and . . . " Mrs. Barnett tried to explain that Bo was a "digger," but Ruby insisted the dog would be just fine, and reminded her that the store was only a short distance away. "You can check on him from time to time."

"But we keep him busy taking him for walks and giving him a lot of attention. I won't have anyone doing that while I'm at the store," explained Mrs. Barnett.

"He will find things to do," replied Ruby with a smile.

"That's what scares me," thought Mrs. Barnett, remembering the times Bo dug under her backyard fence before she had big rocks put around the bottom and how she gave up having flower beds after Bo destroyed them.

The shop's door opened. Pushing strands of blondish-grey hair into place, she smoothed down her red sweater with an appliquéd snowman and a brightly jeweled Christmas tree before greeting her first customer.

"Good morning," she said, giving a bright smile.

The man nodded and walked past her on his way to the coffee bar.

Becky, a petite, dark-haired girl, managed that part of the store, and as she made him a cup of coffee another customer entered. When Mrs. Barnett greeted her, the lady walked past her, answering back that she was in a hurry but had to stop for a cup of coffee.

Looking at her watch, Mrs. Barnett assumed these were local people on their way to work. The tourists would probably arrive later.

Becky stayed busy as more people ordered beverages. Most of them preferred regular coffee. After the customers left, Becky called out to Mrs. Barnett, "When the tourists arrive we'll have more orders for gourmet coffees."

"Do you need me to help you with anything?" questioned Mrs. Barnett.

"No, I am fine," Becky answered as she brought Mrs. Barnett a cup of coffee.

"Oh, thank you." Mrs. Barnett beamed, appreciating Becky's thoughtfulness.

"Karen will be here in a few minutes to take over the cash register. I can handle everything

until she arrives if you want to check on Bo," Becky said.

"That's a great idea," replied Mrs. Barnett, holding her coffee and grabbing her purse with her other hand.

Arriving at the Camerons' house, she was glad to see the fenced front yard was safe and sound. The ficus tree was intact and Ruby's plants had not been disturbed. Watching from the car window, Mrs. Barnett saw Bo sleeping next to his empty food container and half-full water bowl.

"He ate his dog food, drank some water, and fell asleep," said Mrs. Barnett, relieved, reminding herself that she had filled both of them before she left. Not wanting to awaken him, she remained in the car and watched Bo's chest slowly rise and fall in undisturbed sleep.

"Let a sleeping dog lie," she commented as she returned to the store.

"This is quite a challenge," she told herself. "I came to see friends and since I was only staying a few days, I brought Bo. Now, I'm running a store, trying to keep Bo out of mischief, and extending my visit for I don't know how long."

As her thoughts continued, she acknowledged she was excited about managing the store and flattered the Camerons had confidence in her ability to do it, but Ruby had no idea what a nuisance Bo could be. Her neighbors and friends in Argyle were certainly aware of the messes he could get into.

Heaving a sigh, she hoped that Bo would behave. If some of her friends attending the Christmas Stroll stopped by the Strawberry Patch, perhaps she could ask them to lend her a hand.

Suddenly an impulse hit her. Quickly she turned into the parking area of a small shopping center. Opening her purse, she took out her cell phone and called Jody Bell, a neighbor who planned to attend a ceramics workshop here this weekend. There was no answer, but Mrs. Barnett left a message on the answering machine giving Jody directions where to find her, and ending with, "I really need to see you."

Next she called the Altoms, who planned to attend the Christmas Stroll. Andrea, their energetic ten-year-old, frequently visited Mrs. Barnett's house to take Bo for walks.

She talked to Andrea's mother and learned that since they had a conflict in plans they would not be attending this year.

Disappointed that she hadn't found anyone to help her with Bo, Mrs. Barnett started up the car engine and headed for the store.

On her way, she remembered that Ruby had told her that her assistant, Karen, had two youngsters, Mike and Jennifer. She wondered if they would take Bo for some walks to keep him busy and out of trouble.

CHAPTER 2

Meeting Santa Claus

When Mrs. Barnett returned, she found several customers gathered around a lady who was obviously upset. Concerned that something might have happened while she was gone, she introduced herself.

"I am May Barnett and am managing the store for the Camerons while they are out of town. Is there something I can do for you?"

When the lady turned toward her, Mrs. Barnett saw that her large, brown eyes were filled with tears.

"Oh, I wish you could. The police just left my house. It happened so fast . . . I was just taking the kids to school and I got right back," she said, choking back more tears. "But when I got home they were all gone!"

"Who or . . . what was all gone?" Mrs. Barnett asked.

"All the kids' presents!" she exclaimed.

"Their Christmas presents?"

"Yes, right from under the tree!"

As people gathered around her, a woman wearing a Santa Claus hat asked, "Your Christmas tree, Mrs. Brinks?"

"Yes, yes," the lady repeated, taking a handkerchief out of her purse. "The police chief is going to meet me here after he completes his preliminary report."

The theft troubled Mrs. Barnett and she felt sad for Mrs. Brinks and her family.

"I am so sorry this has happened," she said.

When the officer entered the store, Mrs. Barnett quickly recognized him as the Salado police chief. His name badge read *Alan Rogers.* He was dressed in a tan uniform with ribbons showing well-deserved merits pinned above his shirt pocket, and he wore a white Western hat.

Walking over to the lady, he said, "I'm sorry, Mrs. Brinks. We checked everything in your house and still don't know any more than we did, but we will continue our investigation as more of your neighbors return from work. In the meantime, we will be looking for any suspicious activity."

"Thank you," she answered softly.

A few customers joined the conversation, giving their opinions of what might have happened.

"They were stolen," declared a man wearing a red tie with green Christmas trees on it.

"Mrs. Brinks, is it possible that while you were busy getting ready to take the children to school one of them hid the presents as a prank?" asked Police Chief Rogers.

"Nooo . . . " she answered, thinking back, "I don't see how any of them would have had time to hide all of those gifts without me knowing it, and besides, my children aren't allowed to take any of the packages from under the tree."

"We checked all the rooms, but kids have a unique way of hiding things in places we'd never think about," he continued.

"I know her kids, and if one had done anything like that, another one would have told on 'em," volunteered a small woman with auburn hair. "You need to catch a package-stealing-thief."

Grateful that Mrs. Brinks was in capable hands, Mrs. Barnett walked over to the front counter, where Karen, a slender, pretty blonde, was waiting on a customer. After she finished, Mrs. Barnett introduced herself and said, "Ruby told me you had two children and I wonder if they would like to take Bo, a happy, high-energy Labrador retriever, for some walks to give him a little exercise."

"Sure. Ruby told me what a sweet dog he was. My kids are getting out of school for the holidays this morning and I'll be picking them up in a few minutes. Is Bo at the Camerons' house?"

"Yes, he's asleep in their front yard."

"Do you want me to get him on my way back and have Mike and Jennifer take him for a walk around town?"

"That would be great," Mrs. Barnett replied, pulling Bo's leash out of her purse and handing it to Karen.

"I'll be back before you know it," Karen said, walking out the door.

While Mrs. Barnett was seeing Karen off, Becky handed the police chief and Mrs. Brinks a cup of coffee. "Compliments of the house," she said.

They thanked her and carried the coffee with them as they walked to the door, which Becky held open for them. After they were gone, Mrs. Barnett caught Becky's attention before she returned to the coffee bar.

"That was very considerate of you. I appreciate what you did."

Becky flashed a big smile before sprinting off to wait on more customers.

Mrs. Barnett stood behind the front counter and began reviewing her to-do list. When she looked up, she was surprised to see a man with a white beard, wearing a red suit and hat trimmed in white fur, standing in front of her. She instantly recognized him as Santa Claus.

"I . . . I didn't see you come in," she stammered, continuing to stare.

"You were busy," he replied with a smile. He placed a large bag of candy canes on the counter. "I will be passing out a lot of these today."

"I am glad you are buying them from us."

She took his money and put the candy in a special Strawberry Patch sack. When she handed it to him, she noticed his kind eyes that seemed to twinkle. He looked just like the countless pictures she had seen of jolly Saint Nick.

"I'll probably be back for more," he said with a grin.

Mrs. Barnett watched as he left, feeling a twinge of embarrassment for becoming so flustered.

Shortly, Karen entered the store with twelve-year-old Jennifer, a slender blonde like her mother, and Mike, a muscular, sandy-haired boy of thirteen. It was obvious Bo was happy to see Mrs. Barnett. He twisted his body from side to side as he sidled up to her and let out a few husky barks. When she tried to quiet him, he only got louder.

Quickly Mike opened the door, and although he and his sister held tightly to Bo's leash, the dog charged ahead of them, pulling them with him. Mike called out, "We'll take him to the park and let him get some exercise."

"It looks like we're going to get some too!" Jennifer yelled.

"Good luck," Mrs. Barnett shouted just as Santa Claus entered the store for a second time. "Back again for more candy canes?" she called out to him.

Santa nodded and walked to the center of

the store, paused, and looked around. "The candy canes are up here by the counter," Mrs. Barnett said helpfully.

Santa nodded, walked over, picked up a bag of candy, and placed it in front of her.

"How much?" he inquired. She thought it strange that he didn't recall the cost or remember where the candy was.

After she told him the price, he handed her a $100 bill. While giving him change, she looked into his eyes. He glared back grim-faced.

Instantly she knew he was not the same Santa.

"How many Santas are there passing out candy canes?" she asked.

"Don't know," he replied, gruffly.

Watching him depart, she wondered why he was so grumpy. The other Santa had been so cheerful.

CHAPTER 3

A Friend from Home

When Mike and Jennifer returned, Bo's tongue was hanging out and he was panting. Jennifer and Mike looked winded too.

"We took turns running with him until he saw a . . . " Jennifer began laughing so hard she had trouble finishing.

"Cat," her brother put in, laughing also.

Sounding concerned, Karen asked, "What happened to the cat?"

Glancing at his sister, Mike grinned and tried to gain his composure, "Nothing. Bo hid in the bushes and we couldn't get him out."

"Mike had to crawl in and all but carry him out," Jennifer giggled.

"Was the cat fluffy, or maybe black and white?" Mrs. Barnett asked with a laugh.

"Yes," they answered.

"Ever since a skunk sprayed him, he's been scared of anything that looks like one."

Karen laughed and said, "I'll take this bunch home, and when I drop Bo off I'll fill up his water bowl at the outside faucet."

Mrs. Barnett thanked them. Then she gave Mike and Jennifer some candy treats.

After they left, it was soon time for Mrs. Barnett's lunch break. Becky told her that she would take care of the front desk until Karen returned. Mrs. Barnett had made reservations to eat at The Rancher restaurant.

Since the Strawberry Patch was on Main Street, Mrs. Barnett decided to walk to the restaurant, which was across the bridge on the other side of Salado Creek and east of the major thoroughfare. The bridge accommodated both pedestrians and vehicles. As she strolled on the bridge between the two metal railings protecting walkers from the traffic and from falling into the creek, she looked down at the clear water glistening in the sunlight, rushing over rocks of all sizes. Mrs. Barnett remembered reading that shortly after Salado became a town in 1852, the people crossed the creek by stepping from one rock to another. In the wider parts, they walked on logs chained to the rocks. The logs sometimes floated downstream when the creek flooded.

Through the years, people tried different ways to cross the creek, but none was as successful as the wire-cable suspension footbridge built in 1868. The "swinging bridge" hung about twenty feet above the creek. Mischievous boys liked to move the bridge back and forth so it would swing higher than usual and make the girls squeal. The "swinging bridge" was used for more than thirty years.

Captivated by the water's movement, Mrs. Barnett lingered awhile. Then she continued to the other side, where interesting stores similar to the ones she had just left lined the street.

"I would like to browse through each one of them," she thought, viewing the art galleries, dress shops, antique stores, and novelty shops.

The aroma of kettle corn and hot dogs cooked and sold by vendors on the street corner reminded Mrs. Barnett that she was hungry. A horse-drawn carriage taking tourists sightseeing passed by. She turned the corner and crossed the street toward a rustic building with a hitching post. A long porch with a wood railing stretched across the front of the restaurant. Mrs. Barnett assumed that, in the summertime, picnic tables were placed on the porch so people could dine outside. While they ate, they could look across the street and enjoy the view of Salado Creek. After she entered the restaurant, she was seated by one of the large front windows with a view of the creek and the lovely trees surrounding it.

The waitress took her order, and Mrs. Barnett kept the souvenir menu to read a short piece about Salado's history printed on the back. She learned that Salado was a stopover for the Overland Stage and Pony Express as people traveled on the Chisholm Trail, and ranchers took the route through Salado to drive large herds of longhorn cattle north to the stockyards in Kansas City, Kansas. She read the names of a number of famous people who passed through the quaint little village, including some outlaws. North Texas outlaw Sam Bass was mentioned. Mrs. Barnett wondered if he stopped there on his way to Round Rock, where he went to rob the bank but was killed in a gun battle with the Texas Rangers. She was familiar with Sam's history of robbing stagecoaches and trains. Supposedly he hid some of his loot in a cave on Pilot Knob, a high hill not far from where Mrs. Barnett lived in Argyle, Texas.

As she waited, she enjoyed a cup of tea and a slice of hot, buttered Texas toast, a thick white bread with more bulk than ordinary bread.

While Mrs. Barnett looked out the window, she couldn't help overhearing conversations about more house burglaries. Evidently Mrs. Brinks' house was not the only one missing Christmas gifts.

Abruptly, a familiar voice called her name. She turned to see Jody Bell, a well-groomed woman with short brown hair, wearing a bright red pantsuit.

Mrs. Barnett brightened up at seeing her friend from home.

"I've been looking for you," Jody said.

"Oh, good, you got the message I left on your answering machine."

"Yes, I went by the Camerons' house and didn't find anyone there but Bo, and so I stopped at the Strawberry Patch. Karen said you were having lunch here."

Mrs. Barnett asked her to join her, but Jody declined,

"I ate with some ladies I met at the meeting, but I will sit with you."

Immediately Mrs. Barnett asked, "Was Bo all right?"

"Yes, Bo was fine. Why?" she asked, taking a seat at the table.

Mrs. Barnett told her everything that happened leading up to her extended stay in Salado and finished by saying, "That is why I am so glad to see you. You can help me house-sit and take care of Bo."

"I planned to be here just today, but I could probably stay a few more days. How long will the Camerons be gone?"

"They were called away to help take care of a sick relative. They plan to have Christmas Eve with their son, so they will probably return Christmas Day."

"Hmmm. I could stay till the day before Christmas Eve, but then I need to go home to my family."

"That will be great," Mrs. Barnett declared, feeling around in her purse for the Camerons' house key. Handing it to Jody, she said, "If you don't mind, will you give Bo some fresh water and a little attention?"

"Yes," she answered. "Fortunately I brought my overnight bag, but I still need to buy a few things."

"Wait until you see what I have that you can borrow. On the bright side, this will give us both an excuse to buy some new clothes."

"I can handle that," Jody replied with a grin, waving goodbye.

Jody left as the waitress brought Mrs. Barnett's barbecue plate lunch of sliced beef, potato salad, ranch beans, and peach cobbler.

When she finished eating, Mrs. Barnett briskly walked back to the Strawberry Patch. She returned just as Police Chief Rogers entered the store. "Hello again," she called.

He walked over to greet her and she asked, "Is it true that more homes were hit by the Christmas bandit?"

"Yes, and when we catch him, he will be doing some jail time, whether it's Christmas or not."

CHAPTER 4

Bo Makes New Friends

Jody rushed through the Strawberry Patch door, pushing Bo inside. Mrs. Barnett gasped, hardly believing her eyes. The black dog's body and legs were covered with red, green, and blue Christmas-tree lights.

"He must have rolled in them," Jody announced, holding the dog's collar and guiding him in Mrs. Barnett's direction.

Happy to see her, Bo wagged his tail, twisting his body from side to side as a concert of lights clanked together.

Stunned by what she was seeing, Mrs. Barnett blurted out, "Where in the world did you get Christmas lights?"

"They must have been somewhere in the yard."

"Oh, that's impossible. I made sure there

was nothing he could get into. Could he have followed you into the house?"

"I didn't go inside. I found him standing in the front yard like this and rushed him over here."

Becky observed the commotion from the coffee bar and couldn't hide her amusement. "Mike said he wanted to decorate the store. He just didn't know Bo would do it for him."

Mrs. Barnett and Jody knelt down to remove the lights, and Karen walked over to help. Showing his friendliness, Bo immediately started wagging his tail, wiggling his whole body.

"Hold still!" scolded Mrs. Barnett.

"It's hardly been any time since I left him. How did he do this?" Karen exclaimed.

"Bo is a pro at getting into mischief," Mrs. Barnett remarked with a sigh.

As they untangled the lights, Jody explained to Karen what had happened.

"And I am positive I took everything out of the front yard that Bo could get into," Mrs. Barnett repeated.

Upon seeing Police Chief Rogers standing outside the door, Mrs. Barnett suggested they move Bo to another location.

"Okay, but let us do it while you stay at the cash register," Jody said, as Karen helped her guide Bo away from the entrance.

On his way to the coffee bar, Chief Rogers stopped to watch Jody and Karen remove Christmas lights from around Bo's body.

Kneeling down and unwinding a few lights at a time before passing them to Karen, Jody explained, "I know he doesn't look like it, but he is famous for helping the Argyle police catch criminals."

Looking unconvinced, Chief Rogers grinned as Jody recounted more of Bo's accomplishments, "He stopped a burglar from breaking into a restaurant in Argyle, and recently he helped the Newton County sheriff catch an arsonist."

When the police chief reached over to pet the dog's head, he was greeted with friendly barking and lots of tail wagging.

Mrs. Barnett rushed to reprimand the black Lab, but her presence only encouraged him to get louder. Using a gesture to halt traffic, Chief Rogers raised the palm of his hand and firmly commanded, "No." Bo stopped immediately.

Mrs. Barnett thanked him, appreciating his help. Then she explained, "He gets started barking sometimes and can't seem to stop."

"Is he your dog?" asked the chief, rubbing Bo's head.

"Yes and no," she replied. "He is really my son's dog while he is on a government job in Alaska, but I'm Bo's caretaker until he comes to get him."

"I doubt that is ever going to happen," volunteered Jody.

Mrs. Barnett frowned. "Why do you say that?"

"Because you're always calling him to tell him all the things Bo has done, so why should he take away all your fun?"

Mrs. Barnett tossed her hands in the air, rejecting such a notion. She returned to her post behind the counter. Jody laughed, knowing that Mrs. Barnett didn't think all of Bo's shenanigans were funny.

As Santa Claus entered the store, Mrs. Barnett greeted him. "Are you already out of candy canes?"

Looking into his eyes, she immediately recognized him to be the same man who had been in the store only a short while ago. Studying him more carefully, she thought he looked thinner than the first, friendlier Santa.

Shaking his head, the man dressed as Santa proceeded to the coffee bar but stopped to watch Jody and Karen remove the Christmas-tree lights from Bo.

"The dog wanted to get into the Christmas spirit," Police Chief Rogers said with a laugh as he walked past him with a cup of coffee toward Bo.

Upon seeing the police chief coming his way, Bo barked and bounced on his front legs. Suddenly he stopped and fixed his eyes upon Santa. When the man dressed in the red suit moved in his direction, Bo produced a low growl.

Right away, Santa drew a dog biscuit out of his pocket and stretched out his arm, offering the treat to Bo. Bo turned his head away, refusing to take it. Chief Rogers got the biscuit from Santa and moved it closer to the dog's mouth.

Bo's eyes stayed on Santa as if he didn't trust him, thought Mrs. Barnett, watching from her position behind the counter.

"The outfit spooks him," Santa remarked, walking away.

Once Santa was out of view, Bo returned to his friendly, tail-wagging personality.

"You're a good boy," Chief Rogers said with a grin, giving Bo a robust rub on the head before going to the checkout counter. He waited until Mrs. Barnett finished taking care of a customer.

"I understand Bo has had some success in helping law-enforcement agencies solve a number of burglary cases," Chief Rogers said.

"Yes, he has. Despite his faults, he is very good at helping police solve crimes," Mrs. Barnett answered, waving goodbye to the hastily departing Santa.

Santa nodded as he walked out the door carrying a cup of coffee.

"That Santa is different," noted Mrs. Barnett, uncertain if she should tell the police chief about her suspicion of there being two Santa Clauses, but deciding to wait until she knew more.

"Yes, he's edgy around dogs, but a lot of people are," Chief Rogers answered. "Would you like to have Bo taken off your hands for a few hours?"

Her eyes brightened. "Would I ever! I was just wondering how I could keep him occupied."

"Yes," added Jody, joining in the conversation. "I have some things I need to do."

"I spent my break time taking off Christmas-tree lights, and my kids are busy most of the afternoon," Karen said, pulling Bo's leash out of her pocket and giving it to the police chief.

When Chief Rogers commanded Bo to "sit," he responded immediately. He hooked the leash to Bo's collar and told Mrs. Barnett they would return in a couple of hours. When he ordered Bo to "heel," the black dog moved next to the police chief's left shoe and walked beside him.

Amazed at what they were seeing, the three of them watched as Bo snapped into step. "Look, he's acting as if he is a well-trained dog!" exclaimed Mrs. Barnett.

"You don't have to worry about him getting into mischief," giggled Karen.

"And it looks like he'll be getting a lot of attention," Jody said with a laugh.

Mrs. Barnett was happy that Bo was in such good hands.

CHAPTER 5

The Sniffing Sleuth

As more customers entered the Strawberry Patch, Becky made cups of coffee while Mrs. Barnett rang up sales, answered questions, and replaced jars of relishes and preserves on the shelves that seemed to sell as fast as she could get them there.

Karen filled brightly colored plates with small crackers and placed them in front of the sample jars for customers to try.

"This is so good," announced one shopper, catching the attention of others to taste the peach relish.

Another customer joined in, voicing her preference. "The Hill Country Caviar is delicious," she said, tempting people to try the tangy black-eyed pea relish.

As shoppers nibbled on crackers, tasting the

mouthwatering relishes and preserves, Mrs. Barnett rang up sales.

A number of parents with small children eating candy canes entered the store. One child took the red-and-white-striped candy out of his mouth and pointed to the packages beside the counter.

"Look, Mama, those are like this one."

Mrs. Barnett's thoughts turned to the two Santa Clauses, and she wondered which one had given it to the child.

While Mrs. Barnett worked the cash register, Police Chief Rogers took Bo to Mrs. Brinks' house. Bo stood beside him as he knocked on the door. When a lady answered, the officer asked if he could bring Bo inside to sniff around. Mrs. Brinks invited them inside and told Chief Rogers that her children were at a Christmas party at the civic center. "I imagine all the kids are there," she said.

At once, Bo held his nose high in the air, breathing in all the smells around him. Then he lowered his head and inhaled loudly. The trail led him from the Christmas tree to one of the bedrooms. His nose pointed the way to an unmade bed, where he gave out a short, quick bark.

"Two of my sons sleep in here," said Mrs. Brinks, as Bo ran back into the living room to pick up another scent.

He captured the smell of the other son and trailed it to another bed in the same bedroom.

Bo continued tracking down the scent of each family member until he came to one odor that led him to the front door. When Chief Rogers opened it, Bo ran to the driveway, sniffing the ground as he went. Chief Rogers and Mrs. Brinks watched as Bo backtracked to the front door and then returned to the driveway.

"He could be picking up all of your scents when you took your children to school," said Chief Rogers.

"Or it might be where the person parked when he came inside to steal our Christmas presents," replied Mrs. Brinks.

"Before we make any judgment, let's see where Bo leads us," countered Chief Rogers.

Mrs. Brinks nodded and walked back to the house.

With his head down, Bo continued sniffing the ground, taking the police chief to the backyard. Suddenly Bo seemed to be aware of something.

Quickly sniffing the back steps, he stopped at the door. The police chief knocked, and when Mrs. Brinks held the screen open for them, Bo pushed his way inside, sniffing all around the porch. Following the trail back down the steps, he tracked the scent across the backyard, stopping sometimes to go back over the same ground. After changing directions three or four times, he continued to smell the ground as the scent took him out the gate and to the alley.

There the scent seemed to stop, and Bo gave the impression he did not know where to go. Holding his head up high, he barked in one direction, and then turned to bark in another.

Mrs. Brinks, who had followed them, asked, "Don't you think he lost the trail because the robber got into a car?"

"It looks that way. I'll ask your neighbors if they saw a car parked here about the time you took your children to school."

"You are a good boy," said Mrs. Brinks, leaning over to stroke Bo's head.

Bo welcomed the attention, wagging his tail from side to side and slapping it against the police chief's leg.

Observing the forcefulness of Bo's heavy tail, Mrs. Brinks pointed and laughed. "That could almost be called a weapon," she remarked.

Taking a few steps forward, Chief Rogers smiled and said, "I'm out of the line of fire now."

"I just know you are going to catch who's doing this," Mrs. Brinks declared as she rubbed the top of Bo's head. "What can I do to help?"

"Keep your eyes and ears open to whatever you might see or hear about the burglaries."

"There have been others?"

"Yes, while parents took their children to school. The burglar knew the right time to strike," he answered.

"I had no idea this was happening somewhere else, but I will certainly see what I can find out."

The police chief said goodbye as he and Bo turned to leave.

The two of them walked to the front of the house and down the street to the next house that had been burglarized. It was only a few doors from the Brinks home. When Chief Rogers knocked on the door, Mrs. Hudson invited them inside. Bo followed the same practice of sniffing out different scents and tracking them down.

The police chief and Mrs. Hudson learned that the burglar repeated his pattern of entering and leaving through the back door, and probably had a means of transportation parked in the alley.

As they were leaving, Mrs. Hudson asked the police chief to wait a minute while she got something from inside the house. Shortly she returned with a bag of freshly baked Christmas cookies for Chief Rogers and a homemade red and green doggie biscuit for Bo.

She smiled and gave Bo a gentle pat on his head. "I bake Christmas cookies for my friends, both human and canine."

Bo showed his appreciation by quickly gobbling it down.

After they left the Hudsons' home, they moved down the street to the Strawberry Patch. Chief Rogers wanted to give Bo a break and pause for a cup of coffee himself. Mrs. Barnett was full of questions for the police chief. As he told her what happened, she felt a twinge of pride in Bo's detective work.

"You mean Bo actually identified where the burglar entered the houses and how he left?" Mrs. Barnett questioned. She made a mental note of everything the police chief told her so that she could tell her son when she talked to him on Christmas Day. She thought of a special way to tell him. She pulled a small notebook out of her purse, and with her pen, she wrote:

The week before Christmas,
presents began to disappear.
No one knew why
for the reason was unclear.

CHAPTER 6

An Unexpected Reunion

Police Chief Rogers and Bo walked down the street to the next house that had been burglarized. When the chief knocked on the door, Mrs. Wright, a sweet, blonde-haired woman, invited them inside. Bo followed his same routine of going though the house picking up scents. After he finished identifying the smell of each family member, he went out the front door and traced a trail back and forth to the Wrights' car parked in the driveway.

"Is that where you usually park?" questioned the police chief.

"Yes," she answered.

Hurriedly Bo led them to the backyard. Tracking a smell from the back door to the alley, he raced across the lawn.

"This is what he did at the Brinkses' house," said Chief Rogers.

"We are just sick that all the presents are gone," lamented Mrs. Wright.

"I believe Bo has pinned it down that the burglar used the back door to enter and exit the houses, and it's possible he parked a vehicle here in the alley," he said. "We'll keep checking it out."

Bo nuzzled his nose against Mrs. Wright's hand.

"Aren't you a sweet dog," she said softly, looking down and gently patting the top of Bo's head.

Remembering Bo's powerful tail, Chief Rogers moved out of the way. Surprisingly, the dog only gently moved his tail from side to side, seeming to sense Mrs. Wright's distress.

Chief Rogers thanked her and left to take Bo back to the Strawberry Patch. When they arrived, Mrs. Barnett was full of more questions. As the police chief told her what happened, she again felt a twinge of pride in Bo's detective work.

"Yes, Bo did a real good job," acknowledged Chief Rogers, looking down at the black dog.

"Well, I am happy he . . . " Mrs. Barnett

stopped in the middle of the sentence and Bo barked excitedly as Mike entered the store.

"What a pleasant surprise!" Mrs. Barnett exclaimed.

As Mike knelt down to rub Bo's head, Mrs. Barnett explained to Chief Rogers that Mike and his sister had taken Bo for a run in the park earlier that day.

"Before he got into the Christmas lights?" Chief Rogers asked with a laugh, reaching down to shake Mike's hand.

"Yes," said Karen, walking over to them.

Looking up at the police chief, Mike asked, "What Christmas lights?"

After they told him what Bo looked like draped in the colored lights, Karen added, "And it must have happened just minutes after we left him."

"How did you do it, Bo?" Mike asked, addressing the dog as he rubbed the top of his head. "What about that kitty-cat?"

"What cat?" Chief Rogers inquired.

Mike told him about their morning run in the park and how Bo got scared of a cat. "I had a hard time getting him out of the bushes," he recalled with a laugh.

Karen then told her son, "Bo has been helping Chief Rogers with his investigations of the burglaries."

"Yes," replied Chief Rogers, "Bo has been real helpful."

"I heard at the party about the presents being stolen," Mike said.

"How was the Christmas party?" Mrs. Barnett asked.

"It was nice, but I left to see if you wanted me to take Bo for another walk. Jennifer is still there."

"I would really appreciate it if you would keep Bo occupied," she said. Turning to Karen, she asked, "Would it be all right for Mike to stay with Bo at the Camerons' house?"

Upon seeing her son bob his head up and down, Karen agreed.

"Would you like for me to drive them over there?" asked the police chief.

Looking at her watch, Mrs. Barnett replied, "My break is coming up soon and I can take them, but thank you."

"I'll be seeing you later, Bo." He grinned, giving the dog a robust pat on the head.

"Be sure to let me know when you need him

again," Mrs. Barnett called as he walked out the door.

He smiled and nodded in reply.

Since Mrs. Barnett could not leave the store yet, she suggested that Mike and Bo wait outside.

Mike told her he would rather take Bo for a walk. "Who knows, we might come up with some clues," he said with a sly grin.

"Be careful," Mrs. Barnett warned. She bent over to pet Bo and told him to be a good boy.

Bo and Mike walked outside, and Mrs. Barnett turned her attention back to her duties. When she looked up at the customer who placed a jar of relish on the counter, she thought she recognized the woman standing in front of her wearing a jeweled sweater decorated with Christmas ornaments.

"Jean Porter?" she asked hesitantly.

"Yes," the woman answered.

"We taught together at Riley Middle School!" exclaimed Mrs. Barnett, recognizing the former teacher from the Dallas-Forth Worth metroplex.

"May Barnett, what a wonderful surprise!" she cried, also taken aback. "I was told I'd see people from everywhere attending the Christmas Stroll, and now I believe it," she said with a broad smile, pleased to see her friend.

Mrs. Barnett wanted to talk but could not leave right then. Therefore, she asked Jean to wait for her at the coffee bar until she got a break.

After taking care of the customers standing in line, Mrs. Barnett motioned for Karen to relieve her from the front counter. Then she walked over to talk to the former teacher. A pretty little girl stood beside her and, after giving Jean a welcoming hug, Mrs. Barnett leaned down to talk to the girl.

"This is my granddaughter, Anna Grace," Jean said.

"Hello, Anna Grace," greeted Mrs. Barnett, shaking the little girl's hand.

"We are on our way to Austin tomorrow afternoon to meet her parents and visit with relatives during the holidays, but we stopped here to shop and absorb some history," Jean informed her.

Standing upright, Mrs. Barnett told her, "There is some interesting history here, and I would like to introduce you to what I know about

it. Would you meet me for lunch tomorrow for some real Texas barbecue?"

"Yes, when and where?"

Mrs. Barnett told her she would make reservations and said, "Meet me here at noon and we can walk there."

Before returning to her position behind the counter, she took a few minutes to tell Jean the reason she was managing the Strawberry Patch. Then she excused herself to get back to her customers.

As Mrs. Barnett walked away, Jean called after her, "I am looking forward to tomorrow, and we'll be here early."

Shortly after they left, Mike and Bo entered the store. Mike told her they had walked around town inspecting trashcans.

"Trashcans?"

"Yes, the thief might have thrown away the gift wrapping from the presents he stole. If he did, Chief Rogers could see if anyone recognized them. I thought it might give a clue of who did it, but we didn't find anything."

"That was some smart thinking, Mike," said Mrs. Barnett approvingly.

Mike gave a broad grin as Bo wagged his tail in silent agreement.

CHAPTER 7

The Break-In

Mrs. Barnett grabbed up her purse and motioned for Karen to take her place so that she and Mike could take Bo to the house.

They walked across the parking lot to Mrs. Barnett's car. Mike put Bo in the back and then got in the passenger's seat. Mrs. Barnett slipped behind the steering wheel and immediately began telling Mike about Bo's previous detective work.

"He has helped the Argyle Police Department solve two burglaries and the Denton County Sheriff's Department break up a dog-snatching ring. Recently he helped the Newton County Sheriff's Department capture an arsonist."

"And now he has run from a cat and tackled a string of Christmas lights," Mike joked.

When they arrived at the Camerons' home, Bo began making strange sounds.

"He knows where he is," Mike observed with a smile.

"But he doesn't sound excited about it," replied Mrs. Barnett, listening to Bo's low growls mixed with gruff barks.

"He probably remembers being bound up in those Christmas lights," Mike declared with a laugh.

"You're right, he was tied up," Mrs. Barnett agreed. "But I am positive those lights weren't in the front yard."

She parked the car, and they got out and walked through the gate into the front yard. While Mike unhooked Bo's leash, Mrs. Barnett headed to the house to get Bo some fresh water.

Standing at the front door, she groped through her purse for the key. Then she remembered she gave it to Jody.

Turning to leave, she bumped against the door and it swung open.

"I must not have closed it," she thought as she walked into the foyer.

"Oh dear," she muttered. In the living room, the contents of drawers were scattered on the floor, and a lamp was knocked over.

Turning quickly, she ran out the door and yelled to Mike, "Take Bo to the car!"

Rushing after them, she reached into her purse and grabbed her cell phone. She quickly punched 9-1-1 and asked for the Salado Police to come to the Camerons' house, telling the dispatcher it was a suspected burglary.

Bo and Mike were in the car when she arrived.

"What happened?" he asked as Mrs. Barnett slipped into the driver's seat and closed the door.

"Somebody broke into the house and they might still be there. The police are on the way. We'll be safer waiting a few houses away."

Within a few minutes, Chief Rogers parked a police car beside Mrs. Barnett. She rolled down her window to tell him what happened. She finished by saying, "We will wait in the car until you need me."

Chief Rogers nodded, walking toward the house.

As he entered, Mrs. Barnett told Mike what she discovered.

Before long, Chief Rogers walked outside and motioned for Mrs. Barnett to come to the house. Mike and Bo got out and stayed in the front yard while Chief Rogers and Mrs. Barnett went inside.

"What were they looking for?" whispered Mrs. Barnett, in case the burglar was still there.

"Money, or something that can be sold," the chief replied in a normal tone. "Do you see any electronic equipment missing?"

"No, the Camerons' computer is still here," she said, pointing to a table in the dining room where the laptop sat.

Carefully they went through each room, but Mrs. Barnett did not see anything disturbed except what was done to the living room.

"It appears the person doing this only went through one room," she said. "I wonder why he didn't look through . . . " Suddenly Bo began to bark loudly from outside. "Oh!" shrieked Mrs. Barnett, startled by Bo's earsplitting barks.

Rushing to the front window, she saw nothing out of the ordinary, except Bo facing the house barking. "Do you think he did that when the burglar was here?"

"Probably," answered Chief Rogers, walking over to open the hall closet. "Here's a box of Christmas lights."

Mrs. Barnett rushed to see. "Look, someone was in a hurry when they pulled out a string of lights!"

"Yes," he agreed, seeing the uncoiled light strings dangling over the side of the box.

"I knew those lights weren't outside. Why do you think Bo was tied up with Christmas-tree lights?"

"Evidently the perpetrator wanted to confine him and grabbed the first thing he could find. He probably dumped out the drawers looking for extension cords, twine, or something to use and happened to find the Christmas lights."

"But how did he keep Bo from barking?"

"With food," the police chief answered. "Burglars often carry dog treats."

"That would keep a dog quiet," Mrs. Barnett agreed. Her mind flashed back, however, to how Santa Claus held out a dog biscuit for Bo, and still he growled at him. Dismissing those thoughts, she said to Chief Rogers that if he did not require her for anything else, she needed to get back to the store.

The police chief told her that she could leave and that she could put the room back in order when she got home.

"Is it all right for Mike and Bo to stay here?"

"That will be fine, and it's all right for them to come inside," he answered, adding that he would be leaving shortly.

Once outside, Mrs. Barnett gave Mike the option of going back to the store or staying there.

"You and Bo could walk around town and see what is happening on the streets or you can stay here and watch television. Soft drinks are in the refrigerator."

"I'll stay here, but first I'll get Bo some water," he said.

"Great, he probably needs some," she replied. "Jody will be here soon and if she needs to take you somewhere, I know she won't mind."

"No, that's okay; Mother said she would pick me up after work."

"You can stay here until then. I'll check with Jody to see what she wants to do for supper."

Before leaving, she gave Bo a pat on the head and told him again to be a good boy.

When she entered the store, she was surprised to see Jody at the front counter wrapping glass water pitchers and putting them into sacks as Karen rang up sales on the cash register. She knew that

Karen and Jody wondered why she was gone so long, but they all stayed too busy for Mrs. Barnett to take time out and give them any details. It was obvious that Jody was anxious to know, making eye contact with Mrs. Barnett and wrinkling her brow as if asking, "What happened?"

Mrs. Barnett waited until they had some slack time. Customers browsed through the store and no one needed attention right then. She whispered to Jody some of the details.

"But the Camerons don't have a Christmas tree with presents under it," Jody said in surprise.

"I have more to tell you," replied Mrs. Barnett, before turning to wait on a customer.

Soon she was able to give Jody and Karen, along with Becky, the whole story about the break-in at the Camerons' house.

CHAPTER 8

A Frightening Encounter

When Mrs. Barnett finished telling them about the burglary, she said, "I certainly appreciate all of you taking over for me. Chief Rogers said it was all right for Bo and Mike to go inside and Mike decided he wanted to stay to watch television, if that's okay, Karen?" Mrs. Barnett asked.

"That will be fine."

"Oh, thank you," said Mrs. Barnett. "Jody, do you have any thoughts about supper?"

"Why don't I pick up pizza? I can put it in the back room here and all of you can take turns. I'll take one to Mike and I'll eat with him."

"That is a great idea. Is it all right with you, Karen and Becky?"

Karen grinned, giving her approval, and Becky nodded, saying, "I love pizza."

"And so does Mike," Karen added.

Jody left and Karen went to the coffee bar to help Becky. Mrs. Barnett noticed the empty cracker dishes and the need for more sample jars. She quickly refilled the dishes and rushed to the storeroom to get some more relishes and preserves. When the shoppers thinned out, she gave a sigh of relief.

Behind the counter, she organized her paperwork and was reading over some of her instructions when Santa Claus entered the store.

"I told you I'd probably be back for more candy," he said with a grin, walking over to pick up another bag.

Mrs. Barnett knew immediately he was the first, more pleasant Santa. She also noticed he was larger than the other one.

"Tell me something," Mrs. Barnett began, "are you the only Santa handing out candy canes?"

"Yes, as far as I know."

"Well, I am puzzled, because a man dressed in a Santa costume has come in here twice today and once he bought candy canes."

"Oh, he's probably doing private parties," Santa told her. "I am the one who is on the streets and in the stores talking to people and passing out candy. It helps to get shoppers in the Christmas spirit."

"That's a wonderful idea," she said, giving him a wide smile while handing him his change.

After his departure, the store became quiet. Mrs. Barnett was looking for a pencil behind the counter when she noticed a set of keys lying close to the cash register. Holding them up above her head, she made them jingle to get Karen's attention. "Are these yours?"

"No, Jody and I saw them, but we didn't know who they belonged to. We left them there thinking someone might claim them."

"I'll hang them on the nail inside the storeroom. If anybody asks for them, have the person identify them first," called Mrs. Barnett, not wanting the wrong person to take possession of them. She put the keys in her pocket to take later.

Before long, Jody entered the store, bringing in boxes of pizza. Mrs. Barnett asked Karen to pass the word to Becky that they would take turns eating.

Jody left the food in the back room and headed to the front of the store with the pizza for her and Mike.

"I'll stay at the house this evening and probably be asleep when you get home," she said, handing Mrs. Barnett the house key. "I got another key made this afternoon. I thought we would need two of them."

"Thank you," said Mrs. Barnett, waving goodbye as Jody left.

Presently Karen walked to the front counter, dabbing the corners of her mouth with a napkin. "I'll take over now," she said.

Mrs. Barnett surveyed the store to make sure she had a sufficient amount of supplies on the shelves before departing to the back room. When she got there, she saw boxes of pizza lying on the table. It was apparent from the number of missing slices that Karen and Becky had eaten.

Following such a busy day, Mrs. Barnett liked having this time alone. She finished eating and was on her way to the front of the store when she caught sight of Santa. From his size, she knew he was not the first, friendlier one.

At this time only, a few people were in the store, which made it easy for Mrs. Barnett to stand by and watch as Santa waited for a cup of coffee. He stared into space, seeming to be preoccupied. When Becky put his coffee on the counter and told him the price, he paid her and walked past Mrs. Barnett out of the store, appearing not to see her.

Suddenly a strong impulse swept over her. Snatching up her purse and jacket, Mrs. Barnett told Karen she'd be back in a few minutes.

It was dark outside, something she had not noticed while inside the store. The cold air made her wish she was wearing more than her unlined jacket.

Hurriedly she followed Santa across the parking lot and down Main Street to a narrow side street. Trailing behind, she watched as he opened the door of a black sedan. When the car's overhead light came on, she saw television sets, computer monitors, and electronic equipment piled up on both the front and back seats.

Her pulse raced. "Could he be the Christmas bandit?" she wondered.

When the car's overhead light dimmed, she quickly returned the way she had come. Approaching Main Street, she felt more at ease hearing the voices of the holiday carolers and people talking and laughing. As the sounds of

merriment filled the night air, Mrs. Barnett smiled. In spite of her disturbing discovery, she thought, "What a happy time of the year."

Rounding the corner to the brightly lit Main Street, she saw a number of people watching the live Nativity scene on the church lawn. She stopped to look at it.

"How peaceful," she thought, enjoying the presentation portraying the birth of Jesus.

More people gathered, taking pleasure in the display. Suddenly someone grabbed her arm.

"Lady, were you following me?" a gruff voice snapped.

Mrs. Barnett recognized his voice, and a shiver ran up her spine. She felt a wave of panic but swiftly steeled her nerves, knowing she had to think of something quick. Now was the time for a cool, reasonable explanation.

As Santa's grip tightened, she answered, "Yes . . . yes, I was. I thought I had missed you when you got into your car."

"What did'ja want?" he asked, squeezing her arm tighter.

With her free arm, she reached into her pocket and pulled out the keys she had found at the store. Jingling them above her head, she cried out, "I wanted to see if these belonged to you. They were left on the front counter earlier this afternoon."

"No, I have mine," he responded angrily, releasing his grip.

Jerking her arm away, she sprinted toward the store. Over her shoulder, she shouted, "If you know anyone who lost them, let us know."

Hurrying across the parking lot, she rushed to safety.

CHAPTER 9

A Quiet Evening

Mrs. Barnett dashed through the door to get inside the Strawberry Patch. As she walked past the front counter, Karen asked, "Did you get your mission accomplished?"

The store was crowded, and in spite of still being a bit shaken, Mrs. Barnett smiled and nodded before heading to the storeroom.

Once inside, she leaned against the wall and sighed. "Whew! I'm glad I got here!"

Relieved that the scary meeting with the unfriendly Santa was over, she took the keys out of her pocket and looped them over the nail.

"These sure came in handy."

Looking at her watch, she saw it was almost closing time. However, the employees could not leave until the last customer was gone, which meant that Mrs. Barnett could not call Chief

Rogers right then. She hastily selected more supplies to put out on the display shelves. Mrs. Barnett took her choices to the shelves and then walked to the front counter. While people waited in line to pay for their selections, Mrs. Barnett operated the cash register and Karen wrapped up purchases.

When the last customer left, Mrs. Barnett was ready for it to be quitting time. The employees finished their duties and began to leave. Mrs. Barnett made her call to the Salado police chief before she was the only one left. Even now she felt edgy. Outside, people were still on the street and the carolers were close by, but they were there earlier and had not stopped Santa from grabbing her arm.

"Safety in numbers doesn't always hold true," she surmised.

Chief Rogers took her call and said he would be right over. After he arrived, Mrs. Barnett described her encounter with the suspicious Santa, while the chief took notes. She asked if she could give a more detailed account the next morning. "This has been a long day, and I am very tired," she told him.

Since she had not been harmed, he told her he would complete his report in the morning. Then he issued a word of caution.

"Don't ever take off and follow someone again. Leave the detective work to me."

"Oh, I will," she said earnestly. Still troubled by what had happened, she asked, "Will you follow me to the Camerons' house?"

Chief Rogers agreed and helped her finish putting the store in order for the next day. They locked the doors and walked to the parking area.

The street was quiet now. Mrs. Barnett got into her car and waited for Chief Rogers to get into his before driving off.

When they arrived, she was glad Jody had left on the outside lights, illuminating the whole area. As they entered the Camerons' front yard, Bo gave a low grumble and drowsily came forward from behind the bushes where he had been sleeping. He arched his back, stretched his front legs, and yawned. Then he walked to Mrs. Barnett and nudged her hand. She had expected him to make some kind of a ruckus when they came into the yard.

"You aren't a very good watch dog," she

scolded. Reaching down, she stroked his back. The dog momentarily enjoyed the back rub before ambling over to Chief Rogers.

"He's sleepy, and besides, he knows who we are. Don't you, Bo?"

Bo wagged his tail and gave a husky bark.

"Oh, don't start that," cautioned Mrs. Barnett and then chuckled, realizing how inconsistent she was. One minute she expected him to bark and the next she wanted him quiet. Wanting to make it clear, she said, "He should bark when someone enters the yard, and he shouldn't bark just to be barking."

Chief Rogers smiled, patting the top of Bo's head. "People are sometimes hard to understand, right . . . "

Before he could finish, Mrs. Barnett hastily put her finger to her lips. "Shhh, don't ask. He might answer," she said with a laugh. Then she told the chief she would call him in the morning when she got to the store.

"I'll probably need Bo again," he replied.

"You got him," she agreed, using her key to open the door.

Bo followed her into the house and curled

up on the dog pillow on the living-room floor. It pleased Mrs. Barnett to see how nicely Jody had cleaned the room, putting everything back into place and adding her own special touch of dried flowers. On an end table, she found a note that Jody had left her. It read:

I think I got everything back in place. Your son called wanting to know if you were all right since he hadn't heard from you. I told him some of the things that have happened and said you would call him tomorrow. Get a good night's sleep. I'll see you in the morning.

The next morning, as beams of sunlight sneaked out around the window shades in her bedroom, Mrs. Barnett awakened with a start. "Oh dear, what time is it?"

Grabbing her robe, she rushed into the hall. The aroma of freshly brewed coffee greeted her on her way to the kitchen. As she drew closer, the smell of freshly baked muffins floated through the air, and she heard Jody taking pans out of the oven.

Knowing that Mrs. Barnett would probably be concerned about sleeping too long, Jody called out when she heard the kitchen door open. "It's only seven. You have plenty of time for breakfast."

"Are you a psychic?"

"No, I know just you and how conscientious you are," answered Jody, placing a plate of muffins on the table and filling their cups with hot coffee.

Mrs. Barnett sat down and reached for an apple-cinnamon muffin.

"They smell heavenly . . . I can't wait," she said, taking a bite. "It's delightful."

"Go slow. I haven't finished scrambling the eggs."

"I'll wait," she promised, returning the muffin to her plate.

Jody put a platter of eggs on the table and sat down. Folding her hands in prayer, she nodded to Mrs. Barnett to ask the blessing, and she did.

Then looking across the table at her friend, Jody asked, "What happened last night?"

Mrs. Barnett gave her an account of her frightening run-in with Santa and her conversation with Chief Rogers.

"He was right to caution you," Jody agreed.

"That man is spooky. Bo sure didn't seem to like him."

Suddenly remembering, Mrs. Barnett jumped up and inquired, "Bo . . . where is he?"

"He is fine. I fed and watered him, and he is lying behind the shrubs, sleeping. When you get a chance, you need to call your son."

Mrs. Barnett picked up her plates and took them to the sink. "I'll do the dishes."

"No, I will. You need to get to the store, and after Chief Rogers picks up Bo, I'll get my shopping done."

Mrs. Barnett nodded and went to her bedroom to use the telephone.

CHAPTER 10

A Bit of Texas History

"Good morning! This is your mother, and Bo needs you. . . . Listen, he is a handful. . . . I know, he always has been, but it's taking four people to stay up with him. . . . Well, of course I am proud of his detective work . . . but he needs attention from his owner, and that's you. . . . "

Mrs. Barnett then caught her son up on all that had happened after she and Bo arrived in Salado.

"Now, when are you coming home? . . . You are going where? . . . The Middle East? . . . Isn't that dangerous? . . . Why don't you take Bo? He is real experienced at sniffing out the bad guys and can keep you safe. . . . Well, ask the government. . . . All right, I will call and keep you up to date."

After Mrs. Barnett dressed, she asked Jody to join her for lunch.

"A former teaching friend from Riley Middle School came into the store yesterday, and so I made reservations for all of us at The Rancher."

"I'll be there," Jody said.

On her way to the car, Mrs. Barnett stopped to give Bo some attention before leaving.

"You are a sweet dog . . . sometimes," she said, gently stroking his head.

When she walked away, he followed her, forcing her to squeeze between the fence and the gate.

"No, Bo, you stay here," she said, turning and shaking her finger at him. "You will get plenty of attention today."

Upon her arrival at the Strawberry Patch, she unlocked the door and went inside. Surveying the shelves, she saw that everything was in place, with sufficient amounts of relishes and jellies.

"That should take care of us this morning," she decided.

Hurrying to the telephone, she called Chief Rogers. He told her he would be there in a few minutes.

After he arrived, Chief Rogers listened

carefully as Mrs. Barnett summarized the things that led up to her following Santa.

"It was my curiosity that led me to trail him. After I realized there were two Santa Clauses, I had a hunch he was up to something," she told him.

Once again she told Chief Rogers about seeing all the electronic equipment in Santa's car and how threatening he had been when he found out she had followed him.

"He must have seen me and knew I would be returning to the store, which made it fairly easy to find me. He twisted my arm, demanding to know why I followed him. I am so glad I remembered having those keys in my pocket."

"You were lucky," he agreed.

"I believe he is the Christmas Bandit, and when you apprehend him, the case will be solved," she told him.

The police chief took notes, and when she finished, he closed his notebook. He thanked her for the information before cautioning her again.

"Mrs. Barnett, don't be tempted to follow a suspicious person again. Indulging in such an activity can be dangerous. You call me instead."

"Oh, I will," she assured him.

Before leaving, he told her he would be picking up Bo later.

"Jody will be there to help you with whatever you need," she said.

When Becky came to work, she was full of good cheer. She greeted Mrs. Barnett, then walked to the back of the store to begin making coffee. Shortly Mrs. Barnett smelled the pleasant aroma.

"Would you like a cup?" Becky called out.

Mrs. Barnett nodded, and Becky brought it to her before customers began to arrive.

Throughout the morning, Mrs. Barnett stayed busy with customers. When Chief Rogers returned, he asked if they could talk in a place where they would not be overheard.

"Yes," she said, leading the way to the stockroom.

Once inside, she asked, "Have you seen the fake Santa Claus I followed last night?"

"No," he answered, "but we have located the other one. He's passing out candy on the street corner."

"He's the nice one."

"That he is. Now, I have your description of

the other one, but if he isn't wearing his Santa Claus costume, he will be hard to recognize."

"I think I could identify him in regular clothes," said Mrs. Barnett.

"Tell me how."

"He is about the same height as the other Santa, only thinner. His eyes are brown and smaller, and he wouldn't have a beard because the one he wears looks false. The other Santa has light eyes, and I think his white hair and beard are real."

"Call me immediately if your fake Santa comes into the store, and . . . don't do any snooping."

"I won't," she assured him, watching him leave.

Before long, Jean Porter, wearing a pale-blue pantsuit with a matching scarf tying back her blonde hair, entered the store with her eight-year-old granddaughter.

"I'll be ready in a few minutes," Mrs. Barnett told her.

Even though it was not time for Mrs. Barnett's lunch break, Karen suggested she leave early, "It will give you more time to visit, and I can take over."

"Thank you," replied Mrs. Barnett, motioning for

Jean and Anna Grace to follow her out the door.

As they walked across the parking lot, the bright sunshine made Mrs. Barnett wish for her sunglasses, although the crisp air and brilliant light made it a perfect day. Jean told Mrs. Barnett that her granddaughter was an avid reader. "And she especially enjoys reading about American history," she added.

"I like knowing what people did years ago, and I like to read stories about their animals," the young girl acknowledged.

"That's wonderful, Anna Grace," said Mrs. Barnett, gazing down at the brown-eyed-girl and noticing how the sun glistened on her long black hair.

The girl looked up and smiled.

When they approached the bridge crossing Salado Creek, Mrs. Barnett told them about the big cattle drives.

"From the mid-1800s until about 1885, the cattle passed through Salado on a feeder trail that was part of the famous Chisholm Trail. Cattlemen used it to take their stock to markets up north. The large herds went through downtown Salado and crossed the creek right

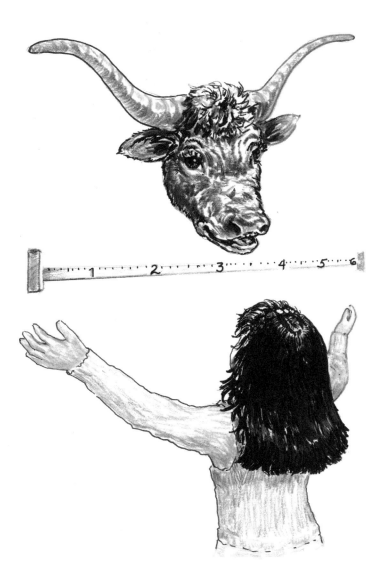

over there," she said, pointing to the water flowing under the highway bridge.

"Were they longhorns?" asked Anna Grace.

"Yes, many of the cattle drives had only longhorns. Their strength and endurance made them well suited for the long journey up north," Mrs. Barnett told them. "The Texas longhorns are important to our history. When the Spanish brought them to America in 1493, they were the first cattle in North America. Later, families came to Texas with cows of other European breeds. These cattle mixed with the longhorns and grew into large wandering herds."

"I haven't read much about longhorns, but yesterday I saw some. Their horns are so big." The girl demonstrated, stretching out her arms.

"Yes," replied Mrs. Barnett, "some of their horns measure about six feet from one tip to the other."

Amazed at the size, Anna Grace spread out her arms as far as they could go and said, "Wow!"

CHAPTER 11

A Daring Plan

After they crossed the bridge, Mrs. Barnett told them some of the town's history she had learned. Then she said, "You can read more about it on the back of the restaurant's menu. They have souvenir copies that you can keep and take home."

Once inside, they were ushered to a front table by a window, just as Jody walked in.

She apologized for being late, explaining, "I waited until Chief Rogers came to get Bo, and just as I was leaving Mike called asking if you needed him to dog-sit. I told him the police chief had him today."

The waitress arrived and gave them menus. After ordering, Mrs. Barnett introduced Jean and Anna Grace to Jody, and then she started telling them about Bo.

"He is a happy, high-energy black Labrador retriever that gets into all sorts of trouble, when he isn't helping the police."

She then told them how Bo became involved in the Santa Claus burglaries.

"Bo was tied up with Christmas-tree lights?" Anna Grace asked in disbelief.

"Yes, that's what we think," said Mrs. Barnett. She detailed Chief Roger's theory about why the burglar used a strand of lights. "He grabbed the first thing he could find and I think he must have kept Bo quiet by giving him dog treats."

"I forgot to tell you there has been another Christmas present robbery," Jody informed her.

Mrs. Barnett gave Jean and Anna Grace the details on what she knew about the mysterious burglaries. "Whoever it is enters the houses and takes presents from under the Christmas trees," she said.

"Are all the robberies related?" Jean asked.

"Who knows?" Jody responded with a shrug.

While Jean and Mrs. Barnett's conversation drifted into exchanging information about the former teachers they taught with, Jody entertained Anna Grace with stories about Bo.

Her descriptions concerning the dog's behavior fascinated the young girl, and she asked, "Bo brings home all the neighbors' newspapers?"

"He sure does," Jody said with a laugh, "and mine is the first one he takes."

When they finished their desserts, Mrs. Barnett told them she needed to return to the store.

Jean said she and Anna Grace ought to be on their way to Austin.

"When we began our shopping this morning, I parked the car right across the street," she remarked, pointing.

They walked to the cashier's desk, and Mrs. Barnett paid the check. When she turned to tell the Porters goodbye, she saw a man wearing a tweed sports jacket and dark slacks entering the restaurant. He looked familiar. As she examined his face, she stopped at his eyes. She quickly caught her breath and looked away.

Noticing her friend's uneasiness, Jean asked, "Is anything the matter?"

"No, I just need to hurry back to the store," she answered, refocusing her attention on her friends.

Mrs. Barnett hugged Jean and Anna Grace

goodbye, promising to stay in touch. After accompanying them out the door, she paused on the porch to watch them cross the street and get into their car. Then she grabbed Jody's arm.

"He's here," Mrs. Barnett whispered. "I just saw him enter the restaurant."

"Who?"

"The Santa Claus burglar."

"Are you sure?"

"Yes, I recognized him."

"Call Chief Rogers."

"I need to get back to the store."

"I'll help Karen," Jody volunteered.

Mrs. Barnett nodded, rapidly taking the cell phone out of her purse. Jody left, and Mrs. Barnett sat down on a wooden bench across from the door to make the call. When Chief Rogers answered, she told him whom she had seen entering the restaurant.

"Stay right where you are, and I will be there in a few minutes," he said.

As she waited, Mrs. Barnett wondered if the man knew she recognized him, or had he even seen her? Then a troubling thought hit her. What if he walked out the door before Chief

Rogers got there? Reminding herself that she had promised not to do any detective work, she considered ways she could detain him until the police chief arrived.

Keeping her eyes fixed on the door, she thought, "I could act as if I didn't recognize him, and ask him to help me start my automobile . . . but my car isn't here. Maybe I could ask him for a quarter to make an emergency telephone call. That's silly—there isn't a public telephone anywhere around. And are the calls still twenty-five cents?"

Nothing she came up with sounded believable.

Her thoughts came to an abrupt end as a group of people walked out of the restaurant. Her eyes scanned the men's faces, and she paid particular attention to what they wore. As the people moved past her to the street, she gave a small sigh of relief. The man was not among them.

Within seconds, a police car pulled into the parking area. Chief Rogers led Bo from the car to the porch as Mrs. Barnett kept her attention on the door.

Overjoyed to see her, Bo whined and licked her hand. Mrs. Barnett's gaze remained straight ahead as she reached down to pet him.

"He hasn't come out yet?" asked the police chief.

"No," she answered, continuing to watch.

"Where did you park your car?" he asked as his eyes scanned the parking area.

"At the Strawberry Patch . . . I walked."

He then suggested she stand on the other side of the porch railing, closer to the parking area. Mrs. Barnett walked around to wait there as Chief Rogers stood on the porch close to the exit.

"We'll both keep an eye on the door. When he comes out, let me know," he said.

Bo sat beside the officer, watching, seeming to sense that he was on duty.

Mrs. Barnett noticed that no one was on the porch or in the parking area. Returning her attention back to the restaurant, she suddenly gave a low cry. Walking out the door was a man wearing the tweed sports jacket and dark slacks. Examining his face, Mrs. Barnett immediately recognized him.

"That's him," she said, pointing.

The man glanced up, startled, then darted to the porch railing. Bo growled, rising up on his

back legs. Lunging forward, he tore the leash out of Chief Roger's hand. The man tried to escape over the wooden barrier, but Bo swiftly seized the bottom of his pants leg forcing him down. The man fell to the wood-plank floor, kicking and screaming.

"Get away! Stop!" he yelled.

The man reached for a wooden support post and tried to hold on, but Bo had the advantage. Growling and shaking his head back and forth, Bo pulled at his trousers.

Quickly, Chief Rogers seized the man's arm and gave Bo a command: "Release!"

Bo let go instantly. Chief Rogers helped the man up and called to Bo, "Sit!"

Hurriedly, Chief Rogers handcuffed the man and walked him to the police car. He put him in the back seat and closed the door. Once the suspect was confined, Mrs. Barnett picked up Bo's leash and took him to Chief Rogers.

He put the dog in the front seat and told Mrs. Barnett he was bringing the man in for questioning.

CHAPTER 12

An Imposter Exposed

Mrs. Barnett walked swiftly to the Strawberry Patch. On her way, she puzzled over why the fake Santa had not left town, especially after he knew she had seen what was in his car. Then she remembered Jody saying there had been another Christmas present burglary. "Maybe he thought no one would recognize him," she concluded.

Jody and Karen were at the front counter, busy with customers, when she entered the store. Mrs. Barnett waved as she passed by on her way to the storeroom, where she hung up her jacket and began selecting more jars of salsa and relish.

Without looking, she knew what flavors needed replacing. She gathered jars of Black Bean and Corn Salsa, Sweet Onion Peach Salsa, and Hill Country Caviar and put them in a cart. She lined them up on the shelves in the store and was returning the cart when Jody leaned over the counter, out of earshot of the customers, and whispered, "What happened?"

Noticing that hardly anyone was standing in line to pay for purchases, Mrs. Barnett told Jody and Karen to meet her at the coffee bar when they were free.

When she returned from the storeroom, they were waiting.

"Tell us," Karen said, impatiently.

"After you left the restaurant, Jody, I called Chief Rogers," Mrs. Barnett began. "While I waited, I hoped against hope the man wouldn't leave before Chief Rogers and Bo got there."

"So what happened?"

"He was still in the restaurant when they arrived. Bo stood beside Chief Rogers and all of us watched the door. When the man walked out of the restaurant, he saw us and tried to jump over the porch railing to escape. But Bo stopped him."

"Good for Bo!" Jody exclaimed.

"Yes, he acted very professional."

"Do you think that man is the burglar?" Karen wanted to know.

"I believe he broke into the Camerons' house and restrained Bo with the Christmas lights."

"What does Chief Rogers say?"

"Nothing yet. I'm sure when he finds out something, I'll hear from him. Oops, people are lining up again."

Jody volunteered to help at the cash register.

"Thank you so much," said Mrs. Barnett, appreciating her assistance.

Shortly, Mike and Jennifer entered the store. They told her they would be gone a couple of days to visit their grandparents. "Do you want us to give Bo some attention before we leave?" Jennifer asked.

"I can take them during my break, and the three of us can spoil the hero," Karen said.

"The hero?" Mike questioned.

"I'll tell you all about it," Karen assured him.

"I really appreciate your doing this," said Mrs. Barnett, beaming. She was happy that Bo would have some company.

After they left, Mrs. Barnett received a telephone call from the police chief. He told her that he was dropping Bo off at the Camerons' house and that he needed him again the next morning.

That night, Mrs. Barnett and Jody were tired when they locked up the store.

Bo greeted them as they entered the front yard, following them into the house and settling down on the large floor pillow. Jody and Mrs. Barnett went to their separate bedrooms, too tired to talk.

The next morning, Chief Rogers called to say he was on his way to pick up Bo.

Mrs. Barnett invited him to have coffee at the house, and he accepted.

He no sooner sat down than both women assailed him with questions about the fake Santa.

"Whoa," he grinned, raising his hand. Then he began telling them what happened.

He said the suspect's name was Tom Martin and while he drove him to the police station, Martin insisted he had done nothing wrong. After they arrived, Chief Rogers took Bo and then Martin inside the station. Chief Rogers had Bo sit beside him behind the desk and the suspect sit on the other side. As he questioned him, Martin argued that he was innocent. When Chief Rogers called in an officer and told him to search Martin's car, the suspect seemed nervous, squirming in his chair and shuffling his feet.

His movements prompted Bo to shove his head around the corner of the desk and growl. Knowing that the officer would find the electronic equipment in his car, and hearing the growls from the dog that helped to apprehend him, Martin panicked and confessed to the burglaries.

Chief Rogers told them that Martin had just entered the Camerons' house when Karen dropped off Bo. After she left, Bo must have heard him and started barking. Martin grabbed the first thing he could find to restrain him. When he tried to confine Bo with the Christmas lights, Martin fed him dog biscuits, but Bo ate them so fast he ran out. Therefore, Martin left without taking anything."

"Good for Bo!" Jody exclaimed.

"Martin doesn't know how Bo got the lights wrapped all over him like he did," the chief said. "He only put them around him a few times."

"He must have rolled in them," Mrs. Barnett concluded.

Chief Rogers continued. "He said he wore

the Santa Claus costume to keep from being recognized. After I incarcerated him, Bo and I joined the officer in the car search and we retrieved all the equipment."

"What about the children's presents?"

"He didn't take them," he answered.

"What!" both women exclaimed.

"Bo and I need to do some more work," he said, getting up and pushing his chair into place.

Jody handed him Bo's leash, and the police chief took the dog and left. He parked his police car a few streets away from Main Street, not wanting it to be in plain sight. After they walked awhile, Bo began sniffing the air as if he might be on to something. Chief Rogers pulled out of his pocket a ladies' handkerchief that Mrs. Brinks had rubbed with her hands. Since she wrapped all the packages that had been stolen from her house, her scent might still be on them. Bo smelled the hankie and led Chief Rogers to an old garage close to Main Street.

He sniffed the ground, running from one side of the garage to the other. He barked at the door, jumping up and down, prompting Chief Rogers to knock. When he didn't get a

response, he tried to open it, but it was stuck. He pushed hard against it, hitting it with his fist. Finally, it budged and he gave it one more hard push.

The door flew open, and to their surprise there were toys everywhere. They were not the kind that can be purchased in a store—they were beautiful handmade toys. Chief Rogers and Bo inspected them and found the tools used to make them. Nearly all the toys had children's names on special tags, and many had labels with notes attached saying, "Return Christmas Eve."

Nobody was there. Chief Rogers and Bo waited, but when no one showed up, they went to the Strawberry Patch.

The police chief told Mrs. Barnett what they had found.

"Bo and I will continue to check the garage until I find someone to question," he told her.

"I am so glad you found the toys," she said with a smile, happy to hear the good news.

CHAPTER 13

A Curious Stranger

The next morning, when Chief Rogers arrived at the Camerons' house to pick up Bo, he stayed to have a cup of coffee. Jody immediately questioned him about why the children's Christmas packages were stolen and taken to the garage.

"And why did the new toys have the children's names on them?" Mrs. Barnett wanted to know.

"I don't have the answers, but I intend to find out. Until I do, I would appreciate it if you ladies would keep this just between us. The public will find out soon enough," said Chief Rogers, finishing his coffee.

"I won't say a word," vowed Mrs. Barnett. "I don't want to tip off the burglar."

"And I won't have anyone to tell," Jody added with a laugh. "I'm going home this morning."

"I can't believe Christmas Eve is tomorrow. The days have gone by so fast," remarked Mrs. Barnett. She and Bo would be returning home Christmas Day.

"When will the Camerons return?" asked Chief Rogers.

"They'll be back Christmas Day, probably late in the evening after Bo and I have left."

Chief Rogers picked up Bo's leash and before leaving, he told Mrs. Barnett he would be coming by the store later.

Bo seemed eager to go. They followed the same routine as before, parking the police car just off Main Street. Chief Rogers did not want to alert the thief.

When he and Bo went to the old garage, Chief Rogers knocked, but there was no answer. Wanting to inspect the building to see if anyone had been there, he hit the upper corner of the door, and it opened.

They looked inside, observing that everything looked the same as it had the day before. Toys were on the tables with name tags on them and the notes seemed undisturbed . . . but as he looked closer, he saw some changes. Bo sniffed around, seeming to notice it, too. The police chief saw a train on a circular track, a new doll, and some freshly painted wood carvings of horses, dogs, and small kittens.

"These weren't here yesterday," the police chief thought.

Bo whined, tracking a scent from the door to a work table with paints and tools on top, then over to the table holding the new toys, and back to the door.

"It's obvious someone has been here," Chief Rogers said, stroking Bo's head.

For a second time they left without knowing who was responsible for the burglaries.

While Chief Rogers and Bo patrolled the streets, Mrs. Barnett was at the Strawberry Patch waiting on customers. Jody dropped by to tell her she was leaving.

"I think I left the house in pretty good shape. I dusted, ran the sweeper, took the sheets off my bed and washed them . . . "

"Jody," Mrs. Barnett interrupted, "you didn't need to do all that. I will have time."

"Who are you kidding?" she replied with a chuckle.

"I appreciate all you have done," Mrs. Barnett said, grabbing her friend and hugging her.

"Glad I could help out. I will call you when I return from visiting relatives. I left your Christmas present on the kitchen table." She smiled, taking the extra key to the Camerons' house out of her purse and giving it to Mrs. Barnett.

"Merry Christmas!" Mrs. Barnett exclaimed, reaching under the counter and pulling out a big cellophane-wrapped basket filled with jars of salsa and jellies for Jody.

After Jody's departure, the rest of the day stayed extremely busy.

Mrs. Barnett was inspecting the cash register when she looked up to see the friendly Santa Claus.

Catching her breath in surprise, she said, "You look just like the real Santa. Every time I see you, I think of Christmas when I was a little girl."

"Thank you," he replied with a smile, placing a bag of candy canes on the counter along with some money. "That's what makes my job so special."

When she started to put the candy in a sack, he said, "That's not necessary. This is my last bag. Merry Christmas!"

"Merry Christmas," she replied.

Chief Rogers stopped by the store later in the day to tell her he didn't have any news, but they would try again tomorrow. He took Bo to the Camerons' house and gave him water from the outside faucet, along with a number of treats he had in his pocket.

Early the next morning, Chief Rogers arrived to pick up Bo. Mrs. Barnett had told him she would be leaving for the store ahead of schedule to get ready for last-minute shoppers.

As the day progressed, the police chief and Bo made numerous trips to the old garage, but no one was there. Late in the afternoon they tried again, and this time an older, white-haired man with a white beard, pink cheeks, and kind, twinkling eyes was inside the garage.

"Don't I know you?" asked the police chief.

"You might," responded the gentleman with a grin, reaching down to pet Bo as he whined and circled the man's legs.

"Does Bo know you?"

"Appears so," the man said with a laugh.

When the police chief questioned him about

the burglaries, the old man readily admitted to taking the presents.

"I've been hurrying to get everything done so that I can take them back, but after your dog found this place I've had a hard time finishing up."

"Why did you do it?"

"To make children happy," he replied. "The old-fashioned way, with toys from Santa, not from a store."

"But you took them out of the houses."

"Yes, I did. How else could I make them better and add some new ones?"

Looking down at Bo he said, "I remember a little boy named Alan who always wanted the toys he saw advertised on television, but one Christmas he wanted a horse carved out of wood."

Chief Alan Rogers' eyes darted to the hand-carved animals on the work table and his eyes got as big as skate wheels.

The old man continued. "I know I shouldn't have taken the gifts, but I planned to return them along with the new ones on Christmas Eve to make the children's Christmas Day very special."

It was important for Chief Rogers to make

sure the old man returned the stolen presents along with the new ones. "If you don't mind, I'd like to go with you when you return the gifts."

"I'd be glad if you would. I could use the help."

"When do we leave?" asked the police chief.

"Meet me here after dark," the old man replied.

"I'll be here," the police chief said.

Chief Rogers and Bo went to the store to tell Mrs. Barnett. She knew immediately from the smile on his face that Chief Rogers had good news.

"You caught the person who took the presents," Mrs. Barnett said, without hesitation.

"Yes," he replied.

"Who was it?"

"The Santa who passes out candy on the streets and in the stores," he informed her.

"And I thought he was a nice man," Mrs. Barnett said, looking disappointed.

"He *is* a nice man," Chief Rogers replied. "The good news is that the toys are in even better condition than they were before. He also made new ones. He wants the children to have a very special Christmas and is planning to return the presents tonight. I'll be going with him. I'd like to take Bo along."

"Oh, wonderful, of course you can," she replied happily.

That evening, the police chief and Bo helped the old man deliver the packages to the front porches of all the houses.

Afterward, Chief Rogers returned Bo to the Camerons' house and told Mrs. Barnett about their Christmas Eve mission. "Bo even carried some of the packages," he recounted with a laugh.

"Did you arrest the thief?" asked Mrs. Barnett.

"No, I let him off with a warning, since he had no intention of depriving the owners of their belongings. And since the gifts are returned in better shape than before and there's even some new ones, I don't think anyone will object to my decision."

"Oh, what a wonderful Christmas!" exclaimed Mrs. Barnett, stroking Bo's head as he sat beside her.

CHAPTER 14

Bo's Citation

After Chief Rogers left, Mrs. Barnett retrieved the notebook from her purse. Before going to bed, she wrote down some more verses to her poem about the week before Christmas in Salado.

On Christmas morning, she quickly got out of bed and went into the kitchen to make coffee. While it was perking, Mrs. Barnett walked into the living room, where Bo got up from his pillow to greet her.

"Merry Christmas, you sweet dog," said Mrs. Barnett, patting Bo's head. He looked up at her as he yawned and stretched his front legs.

Bending down, she rubbed the sides of his jaws. Bo enjoyed the attention, wagging his tail and moving in closer.

"You are a good dog, and it's because of you

that some children will have a merry Christmas."

Before going back into the kitchen, she let Bo outside. Then she filled his food container and refilled his water bowl. After bringing him back inside, she picked up the telephone to call her son.

"Merry Christmas. . . . What do you mean, do I know what time it is? . . . It's seven a.m. . . . Oh, it's just four a.m. in Alaska? . . . That's about the time you always woke us up on Christmas morning. . . . Did you get my package? . . . Good. . . . Yes, Bo and I will be home in time for Christmas dinner. . . . Uncle Chris is coming this year. I wish you could be with us. . . . Bo is fine. He's a hero. . . . The last time we talked, I told you about my frightening encounter with the fake Santa. . . . The police chief caught him, but Bo detained him when he tried to escape. . . . Yes, I'm proud of him."

Mrs. Barnett told him how well Bo performed his duties and how obedient he was.

"Yes, he followed all of Chief Rogers' commands. . . . No, he hasn't gotten into any mischief, but he hasn't had time. He's been kept busy ever since we arrived."

As she continued, she told him how Bo assisted the police chief in finding the stolen Christmas presents and that the thief wasn't a thief after all.

"No, the police chief didn't charge him with theft. . . . I know he took the presents, but he didn't keep them. He had no intention of depriving those children of their gifts. No, he improved many of the toys, and he even made new ones. . . . Bo and Chief Rogers helped him take them back last night. . . . Oh yes, he's a real kind man and seems to truly like making children happy. . . . Yes, I'll call you when I get home. I have something to read to you."

She no sooner hung up the telephone than Karen called asking if she and Bo would come to the store.

"A newspaper photographer wants to take a photograph of Bo and Chief Rogers. Also, Becky and I want to see you before you leave."

"Give me a couple of hours. I will stop by on my way out of town."

Again the telephone rang. It was Chief Rogers. He told her there was a lot excitement in Salado.

"People are overjoyed that the stolen presents were returned in even better condition than when they were bought and that new toys were included," he said with a chuckle.

"That's wonderful!" Mrs. Barnett exclaimed.

"I'll meet you at the Strawberry Patch," he

said. "I have something to give Bo when the newspaper photographer takes our picture."

Mrs. Barnett told him that she would be there. After she hung up she cleaned up the house, packed her bags, and took them to the car.

Before leaving, she left a note for the Camerons and a copy of the poem she had written.

She still had a few minutes and decided to call Jody.

"Merry Christmas," she said when Jody answered her cell phone.

Jody immediately wanted to know what happened,

"Did Chief Rogers find who was stealing the presents? Did the children get any Christmas gifts? Who . . . "

"Whoa," Mrs. Barnett said, stopping her in the middle of a question. "Yes, Chief Rogers and Bo found the kind, old gentleman who had taken the gifts to make them better and to even make new ones for all the children."

Then she told her everything that happened, even the part Bo played in delivering the gifts.

"That's wonderful!" Jody exclaimed, excited about hearing the good news.

"After I go by the store, I will be on my way home. When will you be getting back?"

"About the same time you do. I'll see you soon."

Mrs. Barnett hung up the telephone and made one more check through the house.

After she locked the door, she hooked the leash to Bo's collar and took him to the car. On her way to the Strawberry Patch, she saw people on the sidewalks, laughing and talking.

"What a happy time of the year," she thought with a smile.

Becky and Karen were waiting for her and came out to the car to greet her.

"Jennifer and Mike were so surprised this morning to find presents on the front porch. Did you put them there?" Karen inquired.

"No," Mrs. Barnett replied with a grin, "but I heard a kind, old man made children happy all over town."

After Chief Rogers arrived, the photographer positioned Bo and the police chief for a photograph as Chief Rogers presented Bo with a good citizen's award.

Becky and Karen gave Mrs. Barnett a lovely gift basket filled with jellies and salsas, and a big

rawhide bone for Bo. Mrs. Barnett presented them with their gifts, along with packages for Jennifer and Mike. Before she left, she gave Chief Rogers a goodbye handshake and told him how he had made her stay in Salado an exciting adventure that she would remember always.

"And Bo thanks you for giving him such a nice time," added Mrs. Barnett with a chuckle, looking down at the black Labrador retriever. He was vigorously wagging his tail, enjoying all the attention.

She turned to Karen, asking her to tell Jennifer and Mike how much she appreciated all that they did for her and for Bo. "They were such a big help keeping Bo occupied. Please thank them for me."

She hugged Karen and Becky goodbye and put Bo in the passenger seat of her car. When they were about to leave, Karen ran up and tapped on the car window. "I almost forgot to give you this. It was left at the front door of the store and has your name on it. Merry Christmas," she said.

The tag simply read *May,* and a bright, red ribbon was tied to a carved wooden figure of a black Labrador retriever.

Epilogue

When the Camerons arrived home on Christmas Day, they found this poem by Mrs. Barnett, written on pretty parchment paper, on the dining-room table.

The week before Christmas,
presents began to disappear.
No one knew why
for the reason was unclear.

"They were stolen!"
shouted people, angry with rage.
The police need to stop
this thieving rampage.

They were upset
and all agreed

stealing Christmas gifts
was an ugly deed.

It's unlawful too,
said the police chief,
wanting to stop
the package-stealing thief.

He called to his side
the best dog he knew:
Bo the famous retriever
would find a clue.

Bo sniffed and sniffed,
looking long and hard,
running down the street,
taking a whiff of each yard.

People soon asked,
"Has Bo found a clue?"
The police chief shook his head.
"No, nothing is new."

As days went by
Bo made search after search

until he sniffed the garage
a few doors from the church.

An old man came forward
and said, "I'm all done."
Pointing to the gifts,
"Won't the children have fun?"

"You took them?" asked the chief,
on that cold, winter night.
"I did," said the old man,
eager to make things right.

"I made the gifts better
and built some new—
soldiers, cowboys, and dolls,
to name just a few."

"You did all this?"
the chief asked in dismay.
"Yes," said the old man,
"I've worked night and day.

"They would be returned
along with my gifts